Can Believe It?

Contents

Page 3	Length Illusions
Page 5	The Floating-finger Illusion
Page 6	The Hole-in-the-hand Illusion
Page 7	3-D Illusions
Page 8	The Elephant's Legs Illusion

Wendy Perkinson

An illusion is a trick where something is not what it seems to be. An optical illusion is a trick played on your eyes. Some magicians use illusions to trick their audience. Things are not always what they seem.

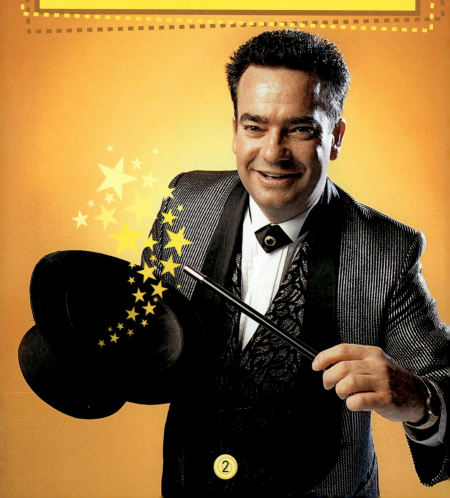

Length Illusions

Try this one with your friends. On a piece of paper, draw two lines exactly the same length with an even gap between them. Then draw inward-pointing arrows on the two ends of the first line and outward-pointing arrows on the second. Now show them to a friend and ask which line is longer. This optical illusion makes one line look shorter than the other – but you know they're both the same.

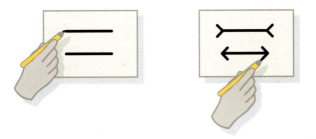

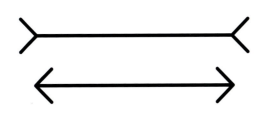

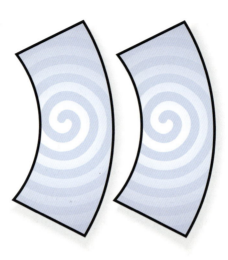

Look at the two cards above. Which card looks bigger? If you use a ruler to measure each card, you might be surprised! Although they're exactly the same shape and size, the card on the left looks bigger. This illusion happens because when we try to figure out the size of the cards, we compare the two curves in the middle. We think that because the right-hand card's curve is shorter, that card is smaller. Our eyes are tricked again!

The Floating-finger Illusion

This is an illusion you can teach your friends. Hold your hands in front of you at eye level. Point your index fingers toward each other, leaving a small space between them. With your fingers in this position, focus on an object in the distance. What can you see? You should see an extra finger with two ends floating in-between your index fingers. If you're having problems seeing it, try moving your fingers toward your eyes.

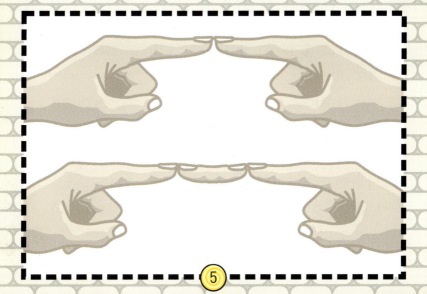

The Hole-in-the-hand Illusion

To make this illusion, you'll need a cardboard tube or a piece of paper rolled into a tube. Using one eye, look through the tube at an object on the other side of the room. Put your free hand next to the end of the tube. Keep both of your eyes open. Can you see a hole in your hand? Is the object you're looking at inside it?

3-D Illusions

Some artists have produced magical 3-D pictures. Most libraries will have books about them, and there are lots on the Internet. To see these incredible illusions, hold the center of the picture right up to your nose! Focus on something behind the image as if you are trying to see through it. Now VERY SLOWLY move the book away from your face and the hidden illusion will magically appear!

Prepare to be amazed!

The Elephant's Legs Illusion

Try this optical illusion. Look at the elephant below. How many legs does it have? Are you sure?

Remember, illusions are tricks. You can't always believe what you see.